This book belongs to

_____

Skin Like Mine

by
LaTashia M. Perry

Illustrator: Brittany J. Jackson

Publisher: Kids Like Mine LLC

ISBN: 978-0-9971579-8-7

Published and Printed in the United States of America

Dedication

To my amazing husband Virgil and our beautiful brown babies; Austin, Justin, Cassidy, Carrington, and Nixon. I am eternally grateful for your love and encouragement. I love you all.
#PerryPosse

Skin like mine is quite divine.
In fact, I'd say it's one of a kind.

I wouldn't trade for any other shade.
I love my brown skin; oh where do I begin?
...

My sister and I are both shades of brown.

Me like peanut butter,
and she a hazelnut spread.
Both creamy and smooth.

If I had to choose it'd be hard for me,
because both are so yummy.

Skin like mine is really neat.
Sort of like a brownie treat!

Dark chocolate brown
so tasty and sweet.
I love my skin from my head
to my feet!

When I look at grandpa's skin,
you know what comes to mind?

Carmel that's it, a touch of golden brown.
Drizzled on top of your ice cream

ooh wee;
this is making my tummy hungry!

My best bud in the whole world Shaun,
we're like cookies and cream.

When we're together
our skin color doesn't mean a thing.
Because, we know it's what's inside
that matters the most.

Color should never keep
two people from being close.

Imagine a world with one hue of colors how boring that would be.

I don't know about you but, I like variety!

Like a bag of lollipops each bringing
a different splash of flavor to my mouth.

If everyone was the
same wouldn't that be a shame?

Skin like mine is quite divine.

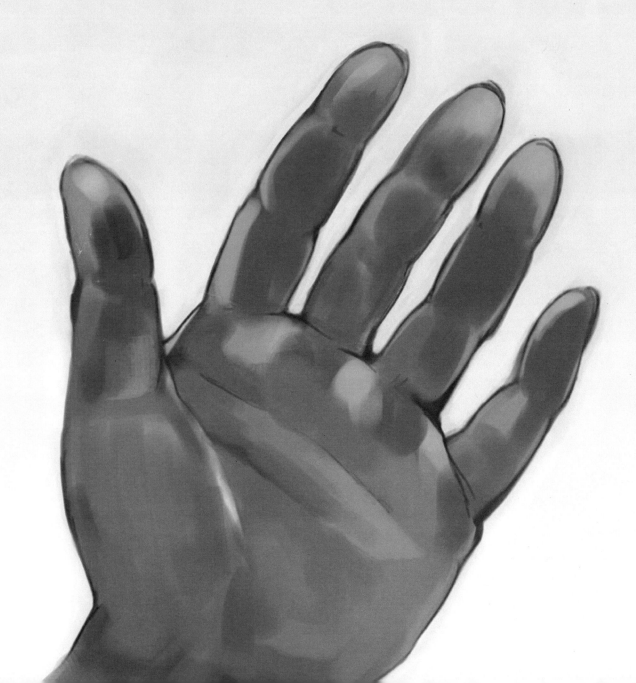

In fact, I'd say it's one of a kind.

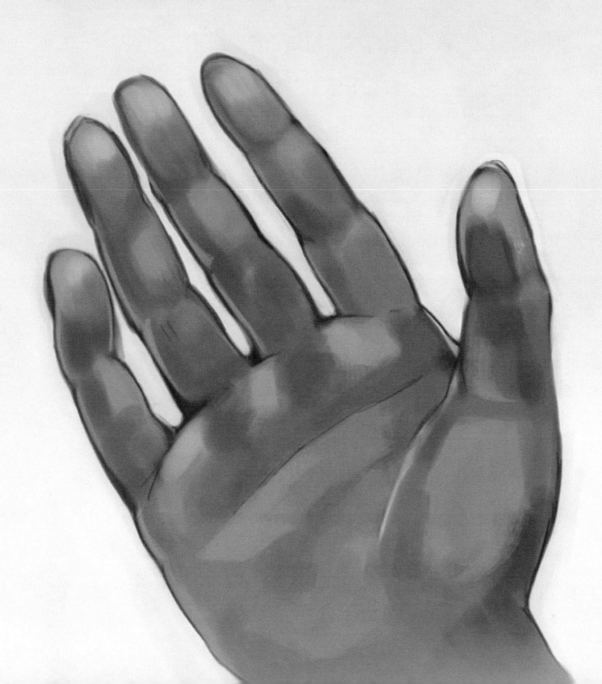

I wouldn't trade for any other shade.

I love my skin.
Oh How I Love My Brown Skin!

LaTashia M. Perry has a strong passion for encouraging and empowering young girls and women to love themselves just as they were created. She is very active in her community, starting the natural hair platform Secret Life of Curls. This was created to support and aid women and their children on their natural hair journey. LaTashia continues her work by hosting events, tackling topics such as self love, body image, and self esteem; never turning down an invite to speak at churches, women empowerment seminars, schools, and other community events.

In her spare time she enjoys spending time with her husband and their 5 children, traveling outside of their hometown located in Michigan.

To connect with the author visit:
www.4kidslikemine.com
Instagram: @4kidslikemine
Facebook: 4 Kids Like Mine
Email: 4kidslikemine@gmail

CPSIA information can be obtained
at www.ICGtesting.com
Printed in the USA
LVRC010004260820
664183LV00008B/34